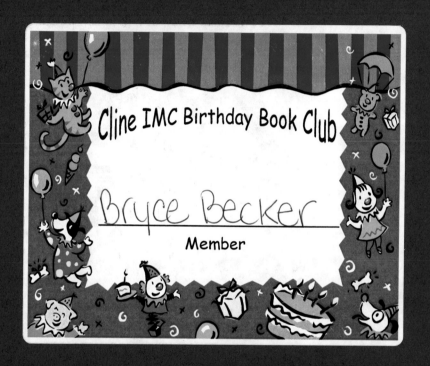

Cline IMC Birthday Book Club

Bryce Becker

Member

Deer Mouse at Old Farm Road

SMITHSONIAN'S BACKYARD

To Eliza Michelle, with love. — L.G.G.

For my sister, Juli, with all my love. — K.B.

Illustrations copyright © 1998 Katy Bratun.
Book copyright © 1998 Trudy Corporation, 353 Main Avenue, Norwalk, CT 06851,
and the Smithsonian Institution, Washington, DC 20560.

Soundprints is a division of Trudy Corporation, Norwalk, Connecticut.

Book Design: Diane Hinze Kanzler

First Edition 1998
10 9 8 7 6 5 4 3 2
Printed in Singapore

Acknowledgements:
   Our very special thanks to Dr. Charles Handley of the Department of Vertebrate Zoology
at the Smithsonian's National Museum of Natural History for his curatorial review.

Library of Congress Cataloging-in-Publication Data

Galvin, Laura Gates

Deer Mouse at Old Farm Road / by Laura Gates Galvin; illustrated by Katy Bratun.
         p.   cm.
Summary: Foraging at night, Deer Mouse narrowly evades a tomcat, but returns to her nest in safety.
         ISBN 1-56899-516-4
1. Deer mice — Juvenile fiction. [1. Deer mice — Fiction.]
I. Bratun, Katy, ill. II. Title.
         PZ10.3.G153De 1998   97-47614
         [E]—dc21   CIP
                                                               AC

Deer Mouse at Old Farm Road

by Laura Gates Galvin

Illustrated by Katy Bratun

Soundprints

Where Children Discover...

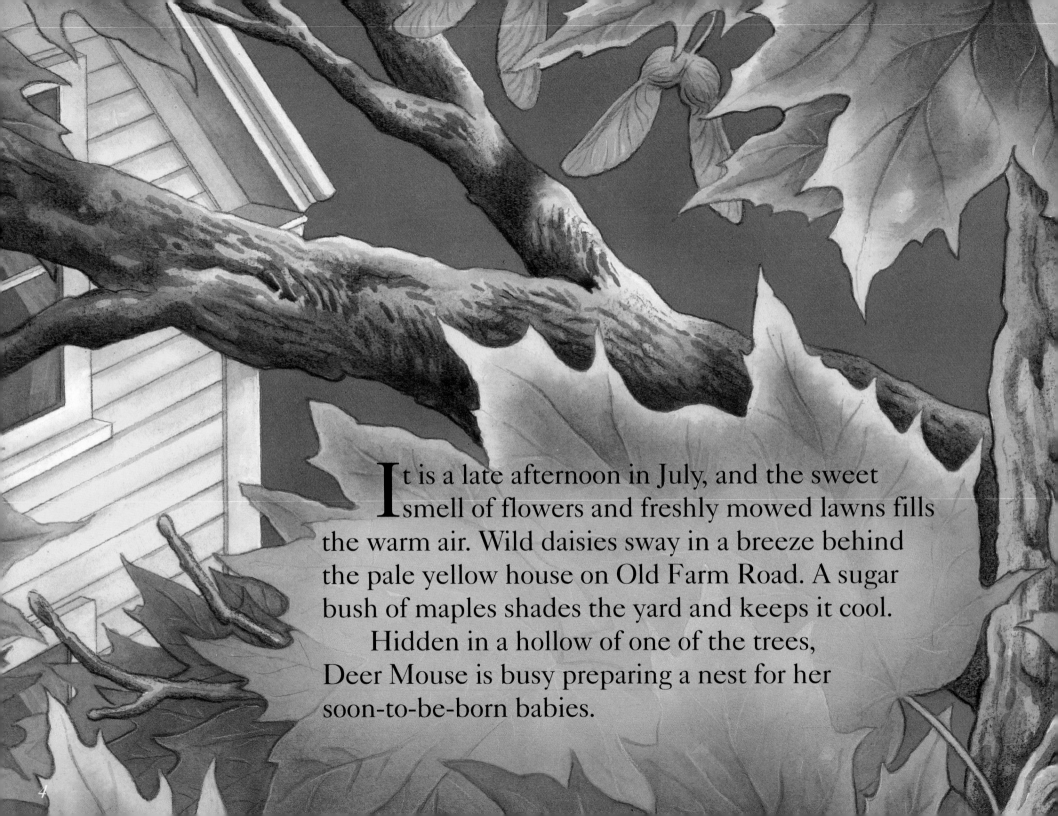

It is a late afternoon in July, and the sweet smell of flowers and freshly mowed lawns fills the warm air. Wild daisies sway in a breeze behind the pale yellow house on Old Farm Road. A sugar bush of maples shades the yard and keeps it cool.

Hidden in a hollow of one of the trees, Deer Mouse is busy preparing a nest for her soon-to-be-born babies.

Deer Mouse lines her nest with the softest
materials she can find—moist green grass,
plant down, and silky dandelion seeds.

When her babies are born, she will cover the
opening of her nest to keep her family safe and warm.
But for now, the nest is finished and she is tired from
all her hard work. She settles down to sleep.

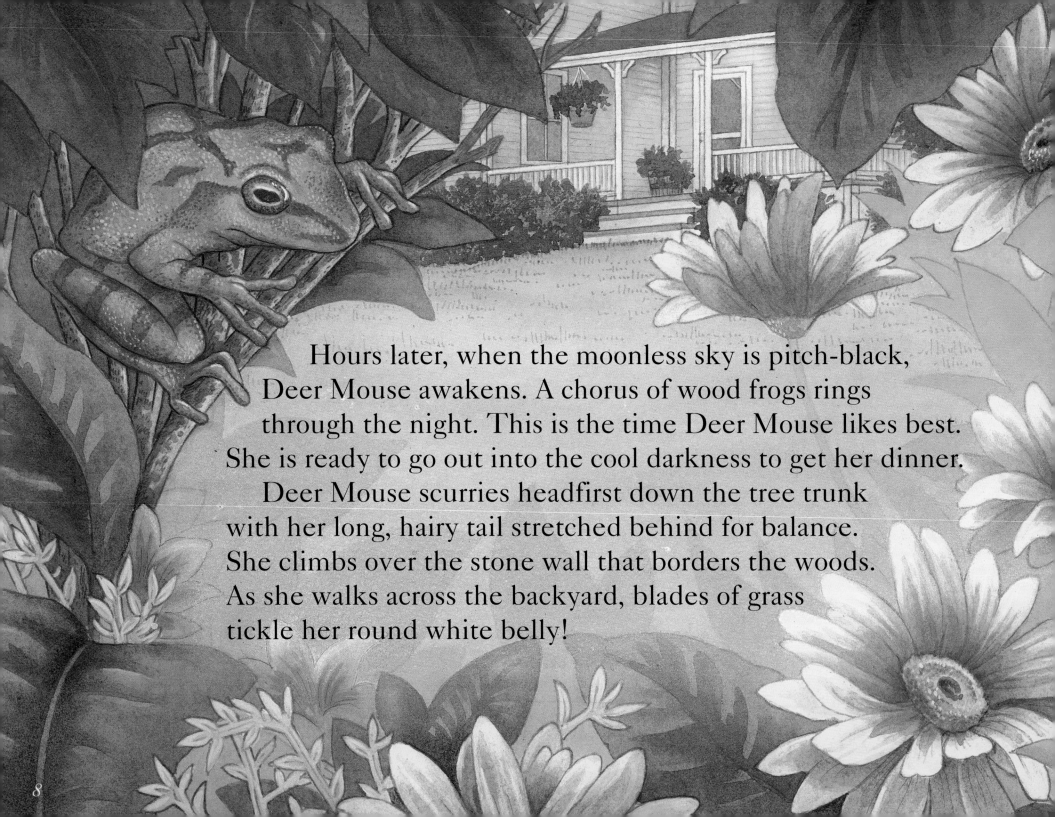

Hours later, when the moonless sky is pitch-black, Deer Mouse awakens. A chorus of wood frogs rings through the night. This is the time Deer Mouse likes best. She is ready to go out into the cool darkness to get her dinner.

Deer Mouse scurries headfirst down the tree trunk with her long, hairy tail stretched behind for balance. She climbs over the stone wall that borders the woods. As she walks across the backyard, blades of grass tickle her round white belly!

Near the back porch, Deer Mouse spots a bird feeder hanging from a young dogwood. The chickadees who ate from the feeder earlier today have left seed scattered on the lawn. It is a perfect snack for Deer Mouse!

Perched on her two hind legs, Deer Mouse delicately holds a sunflower seed with her front claws. Using her sharp front teeth, she shells the seed and swallows it. Then she eats another, and another—one at a time—until they are all gone.

Deer Mouse is not aware that a tomcat has been watching her every move. The cat is crouched down low, hidden between a dense bush and the back wall of the house, ready to pounce on her.

Deer Mouse licks her front feet and washes her face with them. She cleans behind her paper-thin ears and works her way down to her pointy nose. As she brings her feet back to her mouth, she freezes. She hears a rustling sound coming from behind the bush. The tiny leaves on the bush move ever so slightly. There is definitely something hiding there!

Deer Mouse lets out a long, shrill buzz to scare
the unknown pest away. But the bush remains still;
no animal flees. Like a drummer,
Deer Mouse rapidly thumps
her pink-soled feet on a dry leaf.
The cat watches the strange dance
for a moment, before creeping
forward and peeking his head
out from behind the bush.

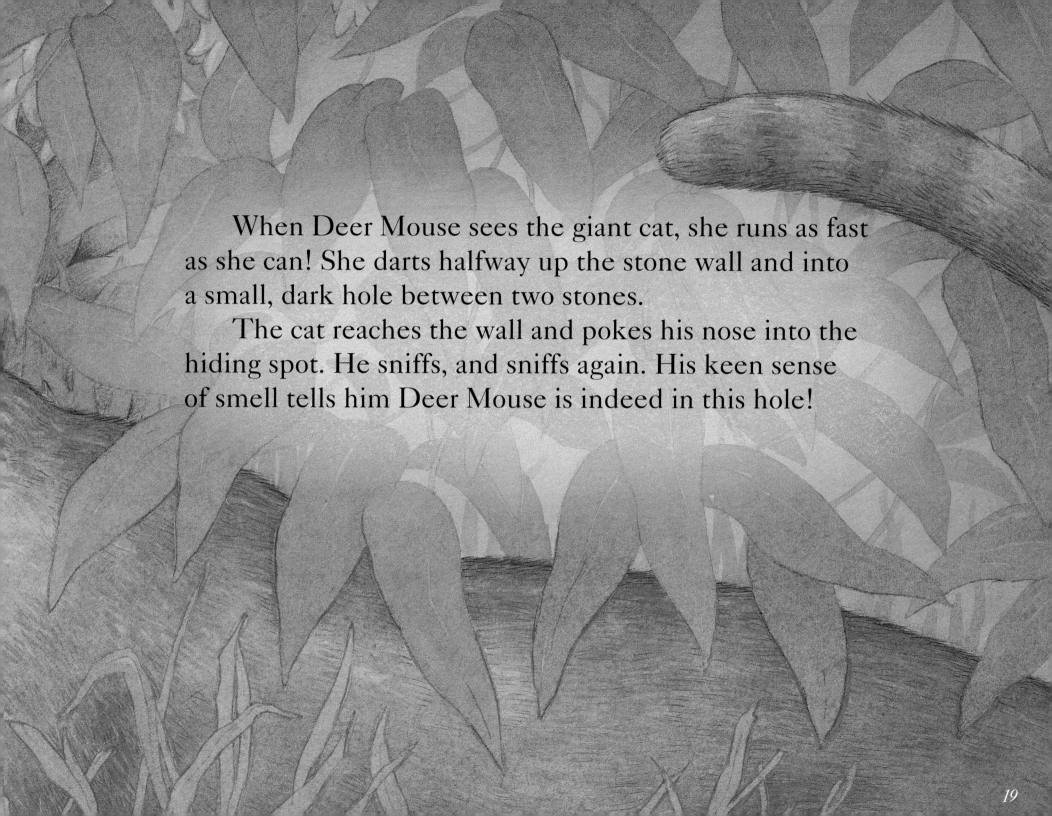

When Deer Mouse sees the giant cat, she runs as fast as she can! She darts halfway up the stone wall and into a small, dark hole between two stones.

The cat reaches the wall and pokes his nose into the hiding spot. He sniffs, and sniffs again. His keen sense of smell tells him Deer Mouse is indeed in this hole!

Deer Mouse's shiny, black eyes stare at him in fear. With a fat orange paw, the cat reaches into the hole and swats at Deer Mouse. She huddles in the far back corner. The cat's pointy claws wave in front of Deer Mouse's face, over and over again. The paw comes close, but it can't quite reach her.

The cat pulls out his paw and sniffs in the hole again.
Frustrated, he tries stretching his paw in even farther.
Deer Mouse is too far back for him to reach. Defeated,
the cat walks slowly back to the house.

Deer Mouse peeks out between the rocks. The cat is gone.
It is safe to come out.

Deer Mouse pulls herself out
of the hole and climbs to the wooded
side of the wall. She walks along the edge, finding
food along the way. In the pouches of her cheeks,
she collects a variety of goodies — carpenter ants,
berries, part of a fallen crab apple. She will eat some
now, and bring some back to her nest for later.

Deer Mouse creeps into the woods. In the distance,
an owl hoots. She stops beside the trunk of a large tree and
listens. If the owl sees Deer Mouse, he will surely make a meal
out of her. The owl lets out another cry. He is far away,
deep in the woods. Deer Mouse is not in danger,
so she continues walking.

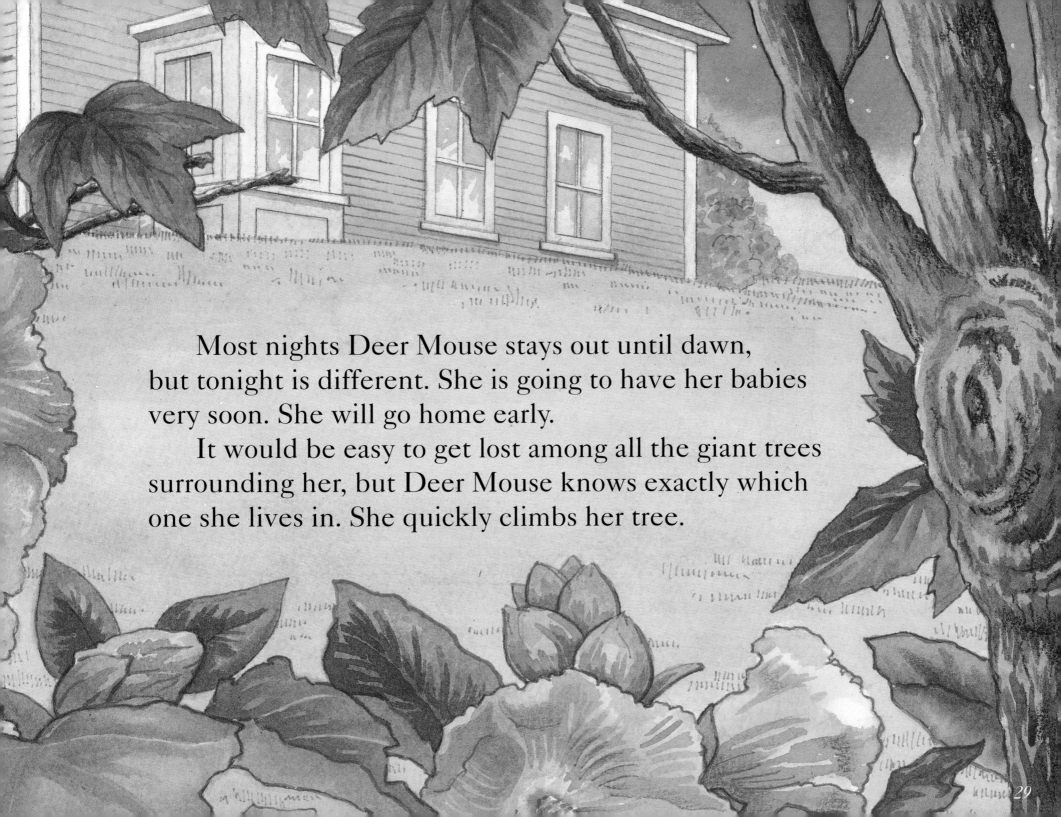

Most nights Deer Mouse stays out until dawn, but tonight is different. She is going to have her babies very soon. She will go home early.

It would be easy to get lost among all the giant trees surrounding her, but Deer Mouse knows exactly which one she lives in. She quickly climbs her tree.

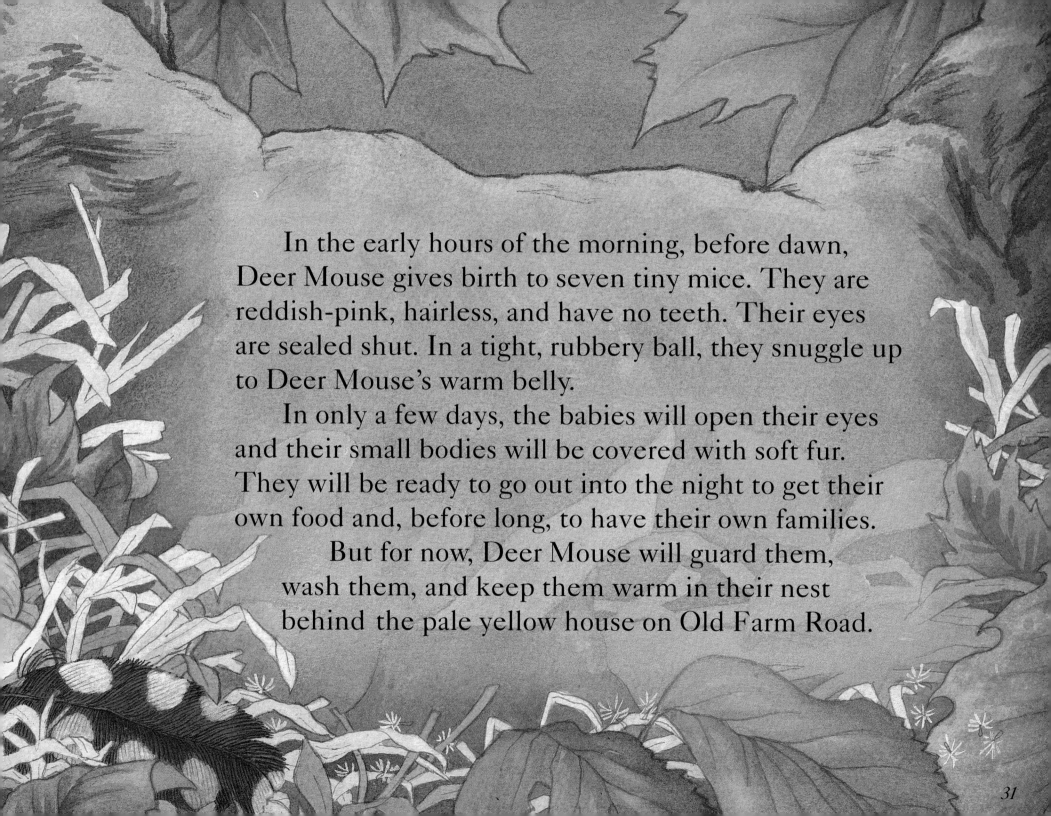

In the early hours of the morning, before dawn, Deer Mouse gives birth to seven tiny mice. They are reddish-pink, hairless, and have no teeth. Their eyes are sealed shut. In a tight, rubbery ball, they snuggle up to Deer Mouse's warm belly.

In only a few days, the babies will open their eyes and their small bodies will be covered with soft fur. They will be ready to go out into the night to get their own food and, before long, to have their own families.

But for now, Deer Mouse will guard them, wash them, and keep them warm in their nest behind the pale yellow house on Old Farm Road.

About the Deer Mouse

Deer mice are found throughout the continental United States (except the Southeast), in northern Labrador, central Alaska, and Canada (except the extreme north).

Deer mice live in a variety of habitats: rocky woods, forests, prairies, or tundras. They will sometimes even nest in old buildings, in abandoned vehicles, or in cracks on rocky mountain slopes.

The average deer mouse grows to be between 5 and 8 inches long. The female will have one or two litters in her lifetime.

Deer mice only go out to find food at night, storing food in their cheek pouches to take back to the nest. For a deer mouse, the dark world is a safe world. They even avoid going out if the moon is too bright.

Glossary

chickadee: a small, gray and white North American bird with a black or brown cap.

dense: thick; close together.

dogwood: a flowering tree with four-petalled pink or white flowers.

hollow: a hole or empty space within a tree.

plant down: soft, fluffy fibers found on some leaves, stems, or seeds.

pounce: to make a sudden jump; to try to catch.

rustling: small, quick, whispery sounds.

sugar bush: a woods of sugar maples.

Points of Interest in this Book

pp. 4-5 maple keys—the double-winged fruits of the maple tree.

pp. 6-7 downy woodpecker feathers, mulberries, dandelion down.

pp. 8-9 spring peeper (frog), ursinia daisies, sweet alyssum.

pp. 10-11 snowdrop anemone, red clover.

pp. 22-23 field poppy, firefly.

pp. 24-25 black carpenter ant, harlequin cabbage beetle, wild raspberries, crab apple.

pp. 26-27 eastern screech owl.

pp. 28-29 hollyhocks.